A Columbia Pictures Presentation

STUART LITTLE™

Stuart Little's Very Big House

Based on the screenplay
by M. Night Shyamalan and Greg Brooker

AVON BOOKS

An Imprint of HarperCollins*Publishers*

COLUMBIA PICTURES PRESENTS
A DOUGLAS WICK AND FRANKLIN/WATERMAN PRODUCTION A FILM BY ROB MINKOFF GEENA DAVIS "STUART LITTLE" HUGH LAURIE AND JONATHAN LIPNICKI
MUSIC BY ALAN SILVESTRI EXECUTIVE PRODUCERS JEFF FRANKLIN AND STEVE WATERMAN AND JASON CLARK BASED ON THE BOOK BY E.B. WHITE SCREENPLAY BY M. NIGHT SHYAMALAN AND GREG BROOKER
PRODUCED BY DOUGLAS WICK DIRECTED BY ROB MINKOFF

COLUMBIA PICTURES

www.stuartlittle.com

Stuart Little's Very Big House

For information address HarperCollins Children's Books, a division of
HarperCollins Publishers, 1350 Avenue of the Americas, New York, NY 10019.

Library of Congress Catalog Card Number: 00-104199
ISBN 0-06-444289-6

First Avon edition, 2000

❖

www.stuartlittle.com
www.harperchildrens.com

Stuart had lived
at the orphanage
for a long time.
No one wanted to adopt him.
He was too little.

When Mr. and Mrs. Little
wanted to adopt a child,
Stuart gave them some advice.
"Don't worry about choosing," he said.
"Somehow, you'll just know."

Stuart was right.
The Littles knew just what to do.
The Littles adopted Stuart.

Stuart moved
into his new home.
It was a nice home.
But it was very big.

A giant white ball of fluff
leaped at Stuart!
It was Snowbell,
the family cat.
Even he was bigger than Stuart.

Stuart met his new brother, George.
George thought Stuart
was too small to be a brother.

At dinner he was very quiet.
He pushed his food
around on his plate.

"George, do you
have anything
to ask Stuart?"
said Mrs. Little.
"Ask me anything,"
said Stuart.
"Can you pass
the gravy?"
asked George.

Mr. and Mrs. Little showed Stuart
his new bedroom.
"Sure is roomy,"
said Stuart.
Stuart's new parents
kissed him good night.
"Good night, Mom.
Good night, Dad," said Stuart.

Stuart woke up early
the next morning.
Today was going to be
a great day.
Stuart followed George
into the bathroom.

They brushed their teeth.
George took off his pajama top
and dropped it to the floor.
It landed on top of Stuart!

George scooped up the pajama top
and threw it into the laundry chute.
But Stuart was stuck inside!
Mrs. Little grabbed the clothes.
She tossed them
into the washing machine
and turned it on.

Water flowed into the machine.
Stuart banged on the glass.
"Mom! Mom! Hello, Mom.

It's Stuart.
I'm in the washing machine!"
But Mrs. Little couldn't hear him.

Snowbell entered the room.

"Snowbell!

Can you turn this thing off?"

"Why would I turn it off?

It's my favorite show,"
said Snowbell.
Snowbell turned around
and walked away.

Stuart scrambled
on top of some socks
and started yelling.
Finally Mrs. Little came back
and noticed Stuart.
She opened the washing machine door.
Out flew water, soapsuds, and clothes.
And out flew Stuart.

The rest of the Littles
met Stuart.
His uncle gave him a baseball.
"How's he going to toss a ball?"
asked George.
"He's not my brother,
he's a little mouse!"

But then Stuart discovered he
was the perfect size
to ride on George's trains.

He also fit in George's toy car.
Now George liked
having Stuart around.

Stuart was the right size
to sail George's boat, too.
He sailed it in a boat race,
and won!

Stuart Little fit in
with his new family perfectly.